what do you do with a DRAWBRIDGE?

by
Dorothy
Wyeth
Dobbins

illustrated by
Dwight Dobbins

⋀ Addison-Wesley

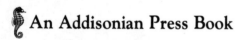
An Addisonian Press Book

Text Copyright © 1976 by Dorothy Wyeth Dobbins
Illustrations Copyright © 1976 by Dwight Dobbins
All Rights Reserved
Addison-Wesley Publishing Company, Inc.
Reading, Massachusetts 01867
Printed in the United States of America
First Printing

WZ/WZ   3/76   01459

Library of Congress Cataloging in Publication Data

Dobbins, Dorothy Wyeth, 1929-
    What do you do with a drawbridge?

    "An Addisonian Press book."

    SUMMARY: A family decides to build a castle to
go with the drawbridge which has mysteriously
appeared at their front door. Includes a glossary of
terms.

[1. Castles—Fiction]   I.   Dobbins, Dwight.
II.   Title.
PZ7.D653Wh   [Fic]   75-8873
ISBN 0-201-01459-9

Some houses have a brown shingle roof,
and there are other houses with red brick chimneys,
and some that have bright yellow shutters.
This tale is about a house with a green front door.

But then, very early one morning, something happened.

On the morning something happened,
Johnathon Jones discovered a surprise.

The green front door of his house had disappeared!
Instead of the door there was a huge iron gate.

Beyond, was a wooden bridge held up
by long heavy chains.
Under the bridge was water.
Water was all around the house, too!

"That is a drawbridge," said Johnathon's father.

"But what do you do with a drawbridge?"
asked Johnathon's mother.
"For surely a drawbridge is rare?"

"And quite special," his father agreed.
So they called up a builder and started to plan.

"Your gate is a portcullis" the builder said,
"and a portcullis front needs a postern rear door—"

In an hour, with sketches and books about knighthood
to follow, they were adding necessities like the bailey,
—and, of course, some towers.

"A banquet hall would be nice," Mrs. Jones thought.
"We must have an armory, right there—" Johnathon's father replied.
The builder suggested the walls be of stone.
"Oh, with torch-lighted halls!" Mrs. Jones added.
"Down to a *deep dark moldy* dungeon!" was Johnathon's shout.

And workmen began that same day
building a house to fit drawbridge decor!

The masons formed parapets,
the carpenters hewed beams,
windows were leaded,

—and a crane came
to lift men and materials high
so that buttresses might fly,
and banners be raised on the towers.

Everywhere was uproar, noise, and hammering.
Everything was construction clatter.
What you might expect
when you're building a castle!

And then it was done. Complete!

The next thing to do was explore the inside.

Through passageways whispering tales of fair maidens.

And of knights, brave and bold,
who defended the castle and chivalrous code—

against stalwart enemies!

And woe to the loser
because of the dungeon below.

While above, amid banquet hall splendor,
knights gallantly toasted the queen—
and ballads were sung of honor and courage
and of battles, well won,
till a trumpeting herald called
"To the top! To the tower!"

They climbed and they climbed.

They went up—and up.

Mr. Jones moaned, "Does that boy never stop?"

Mrs. Jones listened.

"Why here come the neighbors—how nice!"

Johnathon's father climbed higher to see,
then wondered,
"They look mad to me—

And then, up in the sky,

"That spyglass can show us the trouble down there—"

Johnathon swung the glass down toward the ground.
The builder leaned over the parapet edge.
Johnathon's father squinted one eye,
and looked through the glass with the other.

"They're mobbing our moat!"
"They're storming our castle!"

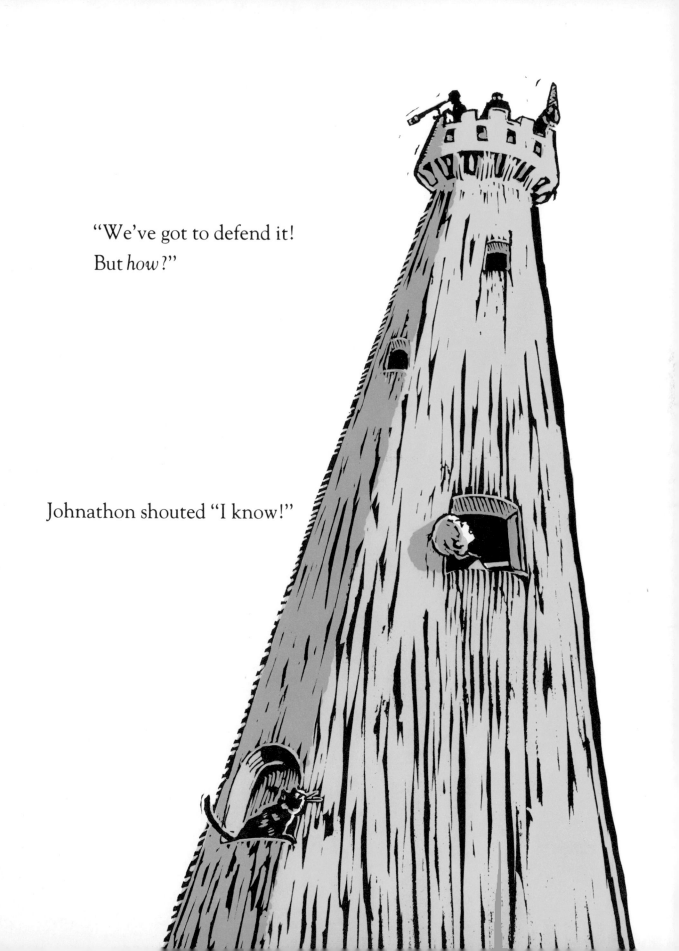

"We've got to defend it!
But *how*?"

Johnathon shouted "I know!"

"Nobody crosses a drawbridge that's up!"

Mr. and Mrs. Jones smiled.

"All things have a purpose," said Johnathon's dad,

"and that's what you do with a drawbridge—"

"withdraw!"

Build Your Own Castle

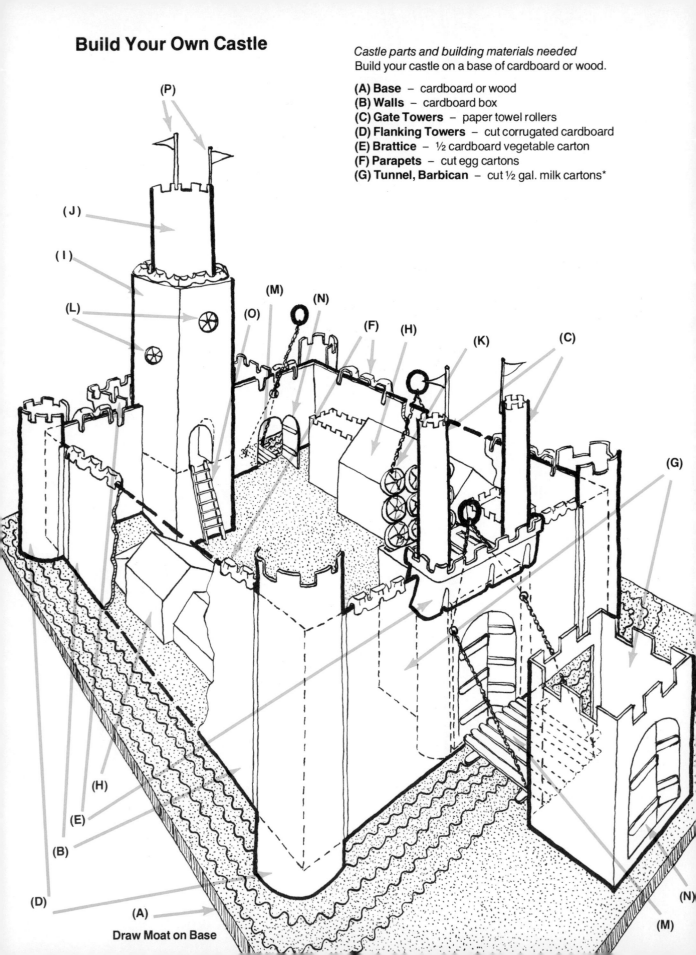

Castle parts and building materials needed
Build your castle on a base of cardboard or wood.

(A) Base – cardboard or wood
(B) Walls – cardboard box
(C) Gate Towers – paper towel rollers
(D) Flanking Towers – cut corrugated cardboard
(E) Brattice – ½ cardboard vegetable carton
(F) Parapets – cut egg cartons
(G) Tunnel, Barbican – cut ½ gal. milk cartons*

Draw Moat on Base

(H) Buildings in Bailey – cut ½ gal. milk cartons*
(I) Keep (lower) – two milk cartons*
(J) Keep (upper) – round cardboard salt box (26 Oz.)
(K) Portcullis – wagon wheels pasta (glued)
(L) Windows of Keep – wagon wheels pasta (glued)
(M) Drawbridges – popsicle sticks and cord (pulls)
(N) Gates – cardboard and popsicle sticks
(O) Ladder – popsicle sticks and toothpicks
(P) Flagpoles – straws and colored paper
*cover cartons with brown bag paper (glued)

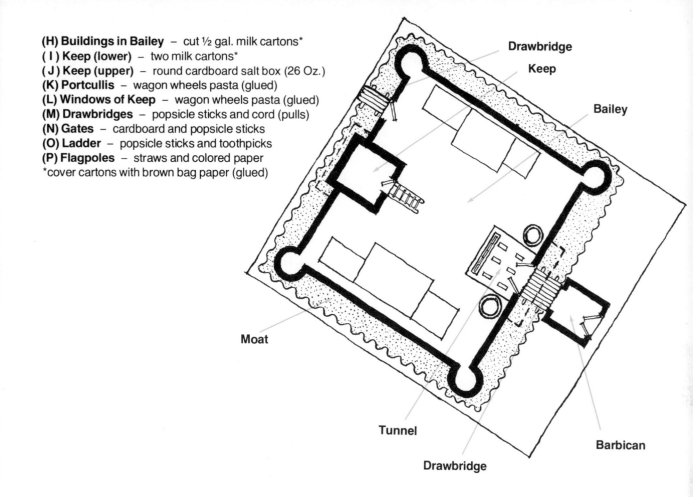

Castle Words

armory – storehouse for weapons, in keep.

bailey – castle courtyard. Location of keep, hall, chapel, palace, stables, food storehouse, and soldiers' housing.

ballads – songs or poems that tell a story.

banquet hall – big room where feasting is done.

barbican – low gate wall outside castle. To hold attack till drawbridge is up.

brattice – overhang from castle wall, with slits. Defenders poured hot oil on attackers.

buttresses – supports against a wall.

chivalrous code – (code of chivalry). Rules of knights: to have honor, be brave, be fair to enemy, respect women, and protect the weak.

decor – decoration; in a building or room.

drawbridge – a bridge made to open and close.

dungeon – underground room for prisoners (keep).

gallantly—respectfully and politely to women.

herald – messenger who makes announcements.

hewed – shaped with cutting or chopping blows.

keep – highest tower. Last stand of defense. Had high up door or ladder entrance. (Defenders could burn or pull up.)

leaded – metal strips holding glass; windows.

maiden – girl; young unmarried woman.

masons – builders using stone or brick.

moat – deep ditch around castle (often with water, but not always).

parapet – low protecting wall at top of castle wall to shield guards' walk.

portcullis – iron entrance gate to raise or lower.

postern – small "back" gate castle entrance.

spyglass – a small telescope.

stalwart – strong and brave.

storming, to storm – attacking.

tunnel – "trap" area between main gate and portcullis. Had ceiling holes to pour hot oil on trapped enemy.

woe – trouble and sadness.

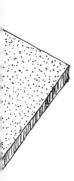

Castle drawing by Dorothy Dobbins

About the Author

Dorothy Wyeth Dobbins is a graduate of both Pratt Institute and the Traphagen Art School. She is presently working as a free-lance interior design consultant and stylist, and has been decorating editor for a national magazine. As a hobby, she has written, designed, and staged plays and puppet shows for children. In writing WHAT DO YOU DO WITH A DRAWBRIDGE? she especially hoped to capture young "poorer" readers and to encourage them to read more.

About the Artist

Dwight Dobbins is art director of a publishing house and has illustrated several books. He is a graduate of Pratt Institute. His hobbies— drawing, and oil and water-color painting — are closely allied to his work.

Dorothy and Dwight Dobbins live in Berkeley Heights, New Jersey, with their son and daughter.